Lily
and the
Lissadell
Ghost

This

World Book Day 2021 book

is a gift from

your local bookseller

and

THE O'BRIEN PRESS

O'BRIEN

JUDI CURTIN grew up in Cork and now lives in Limerick, where she is married with three children. Judi is the author of *Lily at Lissadell*, *Lily Steps Up*, *Time After Time*, *Stand By Me*, (for which she won an Irish Book Award), *You've Got A Friend*, and of the bestselling 'Eva' and 'Alice & Megan' series. With Roisin Meaney, she is the author of *See If I Care*. Her books have been published in German, Spanish, Portuguese, Welsh, Finnish, Swedish, Norwegian, Russian, Serbian, Turkish, Czech, and in Australia and New Zealand.

Judi Curtin

Lily *and the* Lissadell Ghost

THE O'BRIEN PRESS
DUBLIN

First published 2021 by
The O'Brien Press Ltd,
12 Terenure Road East, Rathgar,
Dublin 6, D06 HD27 Ireland.

Tel: +353 1 4923333; Fax: +353 1 4922777

E-mail: books@obrien.ie
Website: www.obrien.ie
The O'Brien Press is a member of Publishing Ireland

ISBN: 978-1-78849-230-0

1 3 5 7 8 6 4 2

22 23 21

Internal illustration, cover design and cover illustration by
Rachel Corcoran.
Internal design by Emma Byrne.
Printed and bound by CPI Group (UK) Ltd, Croydon, CR0 4YY.
The paper in this book is produced using pulp from managed forests.

Published in

DUBLIN

UNESCO
City of Literature

Chapter One

The smell coming from the kitchen was sweet, warm and almost irresistible.

'Custard tarts,' I sighed. 'Cook has made custard tarts again.'

Cook came to the door, jokingly waving her wooden spoon at me. 'They're not for you, young lady,' she said. 'They're for upstairs. Someone already took one when my back was turned, and if I catch them…'

She stopped and her face went pink when she saw who was stand-

ing behind me. 'Miss Maeve,' she said. 'I didn't see you there. Can I get you something? Would you like a lovely warm custard tart?'

'No, thanks,' said Maeve. 'We're just going to Lily's room to get the book I lent her.'

'Sorry about that,' said Maeve as we got to the tiny room I shared with the other housemaid, Nellie.

'That's all right.' It wasn't Maeve's fault that she was part of the Gore-Booth family who owned Lissadell House, while I was a housemaid. It wasn't her fault that she was treated like a little princess, while I had to work hard all day long. We were friends, but

our lives were very different.

Suddenly I laughed. 'I wonder who was brave enough to steal a custard tart? Cook is very kind, but if you take food without asking …'

But Maeve was already flicking through the book. In a world where she had all the finest things money could buy, what did she care about a single custard tart?

Upstairs, Maeve had a beautiful bedroom all to herself, piled with soft blankets and fat velvet cushions. She was lonely though, as her mam, the famous Countess Markievicz, lived far away in Dublin, and she hadn't seen her daddy for many years. Sometimes

Maeve stayed at Lissadell, with her Uncle Joss and Aunt Mary, and sometimes at her grandmother's house a few miles away. It was strange, but I often felt Maeve was jealous of Nellie and me in our tiny basement bedroom with its narrow iron beds.

* * *

Next morning, as usual, Nellie and I had to clean all the downstairs rooms and the dressing rooms before breakfast. As usual, despite the slice of bread Cook had given me earlier, I was ready to faint away with the hunger by the time we got to the kitchen. When Agnes put a big bowl of porridge in front of me, I ate it quickly,

and reminded myself not to lick the bowl clean. When she came to take the bowls away, I waited to see what would come next. Cook was kind to Nellie and me, and always gave us anything nice that was left over from the family's dinner the night before.

When Agnes put down a plate with two small slices of bread and butter, Nellie ate hers quickly, but I couldn't help feeling disappointed.

'Is that ... is that all?' I asked.

'Sorry,' whispered Agnes. 'You're lucky to have even that. Cook is having conniptions this morning!'

'Why?' I asked.

'There was half a chicken pie left

over last night, and she was going to share it out for our breakfasts, but when I went to the larder to get it, it was gone.'

'Are there mice in the larder?' I asked.

'Maybe,' said Agnes. 'But the plate was gone too, and I wouldn't like to see the kind of mouse who can eat a plate.'

We laughed.

'So who do you think took it?' asked Nellie.

'No one knows,' said Agnes. 'I wouldn't like to be them, I can tell you. Cook will murder them and that's for certain sure.'

'Oh dear,' I said, eating the bread and reminding myself how lucky I was

to have any food at all.

Just then Mrs Bailey, the house-keeper came in. 'That's enough chit-chat from you girls,' she said. 'Time to get back to work. The bedrooms won't clean themselves, you know.'

* * *

At dinnertime the next day, Cook came into the servants' dining hall and banged a saucepan with her wooden spoon. I jumped; next to me, Maggie dropped her fork with a big clatter.

Mrs Bailey looked surprised. 'Is there something you'd like to say, Cook?' she asked.

'Indeed there is, Mrs Bailey, and pardon me if I gave you a fright, but

I'm very cross.'

The room was silent as everyone stared, waiting for her to continue.

'Is there any of ye hungry?' she shouted. 'Don't I take good care of every single one of ye and make sure your bellies are full?'

I'd heard terrible stories about servants going hungry in other big houses, but at Lissadell we were very well fed. Every single week, Cook even gave me a big basket of food for my mam and little brothers and sisters.

Only the butler, Mr Kilgallon, dared to speak. 'No one goes hungry in this house, Cook,' he said. 'Your good work and the generosity of the Gore-Booths

makes sure of that.'

'Well then,' she shouted. 'Could someone please tell me who has been stealing food lately? There was the custard tart and the chicken pie, and this morning a fine fat loaf of bread disappeared – and it still warm from the oven.'

Now Mrs Bailey stood up. 'Stealing is very serious,' she said. 'Who has been doing this? Own up now and we can deal with the matter quickly.'

No one spoke. I looked at Nellie and saw that her face was red. Could it be her? Could my friend really be the thief? But then I saw that most people at the table looked guilty. I probably

even looked guilty myself, as I wondered if I'd accidentally sneaked a loaf of warm bread into the pocket of my apron.

'When I find out who the thief is, I'll make them sorry,' said Cook, waving her wooden spoon in the air. 'They'll rue the day they dared to take anything from my kitchen.'

Mrs Bailey put her hand on Cook's arm. 'I'm so sorry this has happened,' she said. 'But I think everyone has now been well warned, and hopefully this will be an end of the matter.'

Cook didn't look very sure, but she let Mrs Bailey lead her back into the kitchen.

When they were gone, everyone began to whisper like mad, until Mr Kilgallon clapped his hands and we quietly returned to our food.

Chapter Two

A few days later, Nellie and I were cleaning the drawing room when Maeve appeared, struggling to carry a big box of paints, an easel and a little stool.

'Come along, Lily,' she said. 'I'm going to paint down by the water, and Mrs Bailey says you can come along and help me to carry my equipment.'

I smiled. We both knew that Maeve had no intention of doing any painting – it was just an excuse so I could leave my work and go with her.

I turned to Nellie. 'Do you mind?'

'Not a bit,' she said. 'I can easily finish up here.'

I gave her a quick hug. She was a dear friend, and never minded when I left my work to go on a jaunt with Maeve.

'Thanks,' I said. 'And I'll make it up to you later, I promise.'

Then I took the easel from Maeve and hurried from the room.

* * *

It was a gorgeous sunny day. As soon as we were out of sight of the house, Maeve hid the painting equipment under a bush, and we ran to the sea, laughing and chatting all the way.

At the water's edge we sat on a rock and threw pebbles into the sparkling water and I told Maeve about the stolen food.

'That's so exciting!' she said.

'It is? I didn't realise your life was so boring.'

'No, really,' she laughed. 'If there's a food thief in the house, then we need to start an investigation.'

Now I understood. Maeve loved Sherlock Holmes stories, and dreamed of being a detective like him when she grew up. (Rich girls like her weren't supposed to have jobs, but I suppose her mother broke so many rules, it was only fair to expect Maeve to break a

few too.)

'Well, I'm sorry,' I said. 'But I think you're a little bit too late.'

'What do you mean?'

'Nothing has gone missing for a few days. I think Cook's warning has worked.'

'Nothing is ever that simple.'

'What do you mean?'

'Maybe the thief is getting more careful.'

'How?'

'Is every scrap of food in the kitchen counted?'

'Well – not exactly.'

'That's it. It sounds like no pies or loaves have disappeared, but what

about things Cook wouldn't notice?'

'Like what?'

'I don't know, do I? Maybe carrots or apples or potatoes or things like that?'

I thought of the cool, dark store-room, where bags of fruit and vegetables lined the shelves. Anyone could sneak in there and take food when Cook's back was turned. I'd heard that in some big houses all the food was locked away, as the owners presumed all servants were thieves. Lissadell wasn't like that. The Gore-Booths trusted us and treated us well. The servants at Lissadell were like a family to me, and I didn't like to think that one person couldn't be trusted.

I felt uneasy.

Was something strange happening?

Something that would ruin everything?

'Come on,' I said jumping up, and pulling off my boots. 'I'll have to go back to work soon and we haven't had a paddle yet.'

Chapter Three

'Stop crying, Winnie. Everything's all right. Lily's here.'

It was cold and dark and as I felt around for my shawl, I heard a sleepy voice.

'Shhh, Lily. It's the middle of the night – and your little sister isn't here. She's at home with your mam.'

I sat up in bed. 'Nellie?'

'Yes, it's Nellie,' came her calm voice. 'You must have been dreaming.'

'But I heard a little child crying–'

'I can't hear anything.'

'It's stopped now, but I really heard it. I'm sure I did.'

'You must have been dreaming. Now go back to sleep.'

I lay back and closed my eyes but it was a while before I could sleep.

Why did I feel afraid?

Why had the crying seemed so real?

* * *

The next afternoon, Mrs Bailey asked Nellie and I to do some mending. As we settled down with a bundle of sheets and tablecloths, Nellie's sister, Johanna joined us.

'I'm so glad you're here,' she said, as she settled down with a lovely silk blouse belonging to Lady Mary.

'Mending is boring with no one to chat to.'

'I'm glad you're here too,' said Nellie with a huge smile on her face.

I still hoped to one day leave Lissadell and become a teacher, but I loved these quiet moments with my friends, and I loved sewing, so I was perfectly happy as I threaded my needle and started to work.

'Something strange happened last night, Johanna,' said Nellie. 'Lily woke up in the night because she thought she heard her little sister crying.'

'Oh,' said Johanna, making Nellie and I look up from our work.

'What's wrong?' said Nellie. 'It was

only a dream.'

'It wasn't a dream,' said Johanna. 'I heard it too.'

Nellie grabbed my arm and squeezed it tightly. 'I don't like this,' she whispered. 'First the food going missing, and now a child crying in the night. It's too scary for me.'

I was scared too, but didn't want to show it.

'Don't worry, Nellie,' said Johanna. 'It was probably one of the little Gore-Booth children crying in the night.'

'But the little ones sleep all the way upstairs,' said Nellie. 'If they cried, we'd never hear them down in the basement.'

Johanna patted her sister's arm. 'You know how little Miss Bridget wanders around the house – maybe she came downstairs in the night without anyone noticing.'

'That'll be it,' I said as cheerfully as I could. 'When I go to the nursery later, I'll tell Isabelle to keep a closer eye on Bridget, so she won't go around scaring the life out of us. Now let's get on with our sewing, or we'll be in trouble with Mrs Bailey.'

* * *

'Thank you, Lily,' said Isabelle, taking the bundle of fresh towels from me. 'How are you today?'

Isabelle, the children's maid, was a

good friend, so I told her all about the crying in the night.

'I think it must have been Bridget on a midnight ramble,' I said, waiting for her to agree with me and make me feel better.

'It wasn't Bridget you heard downstairs,' she said.

'Then it was maybe Michael or Hugh or even little Brian?'

'No, it wasn't any of them.'

'How do you know?'

'Because last week, Michael read a book that was too scary for him and he had nightmares. He was sure someone was trying to take him away, and he gave me no peace at all until I agreed

to pull my bed across the doorway of the night nursery. I've been doing that every night since then, so none of the children can get out of the room without me knowing. I'm sorry, Lily, but whoever you heard crying, it wasn't one of the little Gore-Booths.'

* * *

I didn't tell Nellie what Isabelle had said, so that night she snored as she slept soundly. I kept waking up though. I felt on edge – something strange was happening at Lissadell, and I didn't like it at all.

Chapter Four

'**H**elp! Help! Oh some-one please help me!'

The terrifying shriek made me jump up quickly. I was so afraid I felt no pain as I banged my head on the cold metal bed-frame. In the dim light I could see Nellie cowering in the corner of her bed.

'Was that you?' I asked. 'Are you having bad dreams now?'

She shook her head and pointed at the door.

'Don't go out there,' she whispered,

as I climbed out of bed.

'I have to. Someone could be hurt.'

I carefully opened the door, and peeped out. The gaslight was on low as usual, and I could see Ita and Agnes huddled together in the passageway.

'Shhh,' said Agnes. 'Shhh, Ita. I'm here. Everything is all right.'

Agnes turned to me. 'I don't know what happened,' she said. 'I woke when Ita got up to go to the toilet, and next thing I heard her screaming, so I ran out and...'

Ita was pale. Her eyes were wide and she looked as if she'd seen a...

'I saw a ghost! It was little, and all dressed in white, and it had a big mop

of dark curls, and it was right there.'
Ita pointed along the passageway, but
I couldn't see anything unusual.

'I was so afraid,' she said. 'I covered
my eyes, and when I opened them, the
ghost was gone.'

I wasn't sure I believed in ghosts, but
even so...

Now Mrs Bailey appeared. She
looked funny in her night cap, and a
shawl wrapped over her long night-
dress.

'What on earth is going on out
here?' she said.

'Ita saw a tiny little ghost,' said
Agnes.

'That's ridiculous,' said Mrs Bailey.

'Maybe it was Miss Bridget, sleep-walking.'

'It wasn't!' Everyone stared at me as I told them what Isabelle had said.

'Anyway I know what Miss Bridget looks like, and it wasn't her,' said Ita. 'It was a little girl, but a bigger little girl than Miss Bridget. I know it was a ghost.'

'Enough of your nonsense,' said Mrs Bailey. 'Even if ghosts existed they wouldn't be down here with the likes of us. They'd be upstairs in the fancy rooms, if they'd any sense at all. Now back to bed all of you.'

Before anyone could move, Ita started to wail. 'I'm too afraid to go to

bed,' she said. 'The ghost could be any-where. It could be hiding somewhere, waiting to get me.'

By now Nellie and Johanna and most of the other servants had appeared, all looking tired and confused.

'It was a bad dream, Ita,' said Mrs Bailey, yawning.

'It wasn't a dream, said Ita. 'I was awake, and I saw a little ghost. I *know* I did.'

Then I remembered what Mam used to do when my brother Denis was afraid of ghosts.

'Why don't I look in all the rooms and make sure there's no ghost?' I suggested, wondering if I was brave

enough to do it on my own.

'Good idea,' said Agnes. 'I'll go with you if you like.'

'Very well,' sighed Mrs Bailey. 'Anything so we can all get back to bed in peace.'

So Agnes and I held hands as we checked in her and Ita's bedroom. Like all the servants' bedrooms it was small, and it didn't take long to search.

'Don't forget to look under the bed,' cried Ita. 'Ghosts are good at hiding.'

'Nothing there,' I said, as we came out of the room.

'Thank you, Lily and Agnes,' said Mrs Bailey. 'Now have a *quick* look in the other bedrooms, so we can all get

some sleep before morning.'

Delia's room was next.

'Where's Delia?' cried Ita, when she saw that the door was closed. 'Maybe the ghost got her!'

'Or maybe she's lucky and is a very sound sleeper,' said Maggie.

I tapped on the door. 'Delia! Are you awake?'

As I raised my hand to tap again, the door opened a little and Delia stood there rubbing her eyes.

'Move over,' said Agnes. 'We have to check your room for ghosts.'

'I think I'd know if there was a ghost in my room,' said Delia.

'It could have sneaked in while you

were asleep and be hiding under your bed,' said Ita. 'Or in the wardrobe. Lily and Agnes have to check.'

Now Mrs Bailey clapped her hands. 'I've had enough of this nonsense!' she said. 'Delia, please oblige us and search your room.'

Delia went back into her room, closing the door behind her. 'No ghosts in there,' she said when she reappeared a minute later.

'Johanna, Lily and Agnes, you search any rooms that are left,' said Mrs Bailey. 'If Mr Kilgallon wakes up…'

We were all a bit afraid of Mr Kilgallon, so we rushed to do as we were told. When every room had been checked,

Mrs Bailey sighed. 'Now back to bed the whole lot of you,' she said.

For a minute no one moved. Ita was always excitable, and easily scared over nothing, but even so, I was a little bit afraid. I was glad I had Nellie to sleep with.

Nellie turned to Johanna, who had a room to herself as she was the only lady's maid. 'You can't sleep on your own tonight,' she said. 'Come and sleep in my bed with me.'

I could see Johanna was tempted, but didn't want her little sister to think she was afraid. 'I'll sleep with you if it will make *you* feel better,' she smiled.

Then kind Nellie turned to Delia,

whose room was the tiniest in the house – so small there was no room for any other maid to share with her.

'What about you?' she said. 'Won't you be afraid all on your own? Maybe you could share with Lily?'

I wasn't sure I wanted to share my bed with Delia. At home I shared with my four brothers and sisters, but at Lissadell, I was used to having a bed all to myself. Nellie was being kind though, and if Delia was really afraid...

'I'm not scared,' said Delia. 'I don't think there was any ghost. Ita probably saw a moving shadow in the flickering of the gas light.'

I looked at the flame of the gas light,

burning steady and still.

'I *know* what I saw,' pouted Ita.

'Enough, girls!' said Mrs Bailey crossly. 'You can sleep on the kitchen floor for all I care, just leave this passageway and settle down.'

We didn't need to be told twice. Even Ita was finally quiet as we all hurried to our rooms and closed the doors behind us.

It had been a long night.

* * *

At dinner the next day Mr Kilgallon and Mrs Bailey sat at either end of the table with long faces on them that would turn milk sour.

Ita was pale, with big shadows under

her eyes, and while everyone else did a lot of whispering, she didn't say a word.

In the end, Delia turned to her. 'I'm sorry you were frightened last night,' she said kindly. 'But you only thought you saw a ghost – we all know you have a vivid imagination, Ita.'

I could see she was trying to make Ita feel better, but Ita still said nothing.

'Remember what you told me before?' continued Delia. 'You told me your dead grandmother used to send messages to you and your sister.'

'That was only a game we used to play,' said Ita. 'We knew that wasn't real, but the ghost was real. I *know* it was.'

Mr Kilgallon rapped hard on the table. 'That's quite enough,' he said in his crossest voice. 'There's no such thing as ghosts, and I won't have this foolish talk at my table. Is that understood?'

Everyone nodded, and we went back to our meal.

Chapter Five

'**G**uess who!'

'It's Maeve,' I said, smiling, as she stood behind me with her hands over my eyes.

'How do you always know?' she asked.

'Lucky guesses, I suppose.' Guessing wasn't hard. Maeve's posh voice was very different to the strong Sligo accents of my other friends. Also, her hands were soft and smooth, nothing like the rough, dry skin of a servant. I suppose playing the piano didn't do as

much damage as scrubbing floors.

'What's been happening while I was away at my grandmother's house?'

'It's been awful,' I sighed.

'Is the thief back?'

'I don't know if it's a person or a ghost, but *someone* is haunting the basement, and I don't like it.'

'Tell me everything,' said Maeve.

I looked around, and as I couldn't see Mrs Bailey anywhere, I began to talk. First I told Maeve about Ita and the ghost.

'That's so exciting,' she said. 'I'd love to see a ghost – especially a small sweet one. Has it come back since then?'

'Who knows? No one has seen it

anyway.'

'Oh,' she said, disappointed.

'But the next day I went to the larder and saw Cook holding up a bunch of carrots. I asked her if some were missing, but she just shook her head, as if she wasn't sure, as if she couldn't trust herself any more.'

'Poor Cook.'

'And in the middle of the night, there was a loud crash, and everyone, well the brave people anyway, ran into the kitchen.'

'And who was there?'

'No one – but on the floor was a broken jug and a big puddle of milk. Cook said she didn't mind anyone

being thirsty, but because no one owned up, she was so angry, I thought her head was going to explode!'

'That all sounds very exciting to me.'

'Well it isn't! Everyone is tired and nervous. The smallest noise makes us jump. The servants are always whispering in little groups, and watching each other. Mr Kilgallon and Mrs Bailey are cross all the time. Oh, Maeve – it's terrible. At night my dreams are filled with ghosts and children crying and children laughing, and I can hardly tell any more what's real and what isn't.'

'That does sound bad,' she said. 'But don't worry – I think I know how to help.'

'How?'

'You and I will become detectives. I've read lots of stories, so I know exactly what to do. I'll be Sherlock Holmes and you can be his assistant, Doctor Watson.'

'Why do I have to be the assistant?'

'Because it's my idea.'

I loved that she was so excited, and I was tired of all the tension and fear, so I didn't argue any more.

'Let's start right away,' she said.

I wished my life was that simple. 'I'd love to be a detective,' I said. 'But not yet – first I've got to clean the dining room.'

'Oh dear,' said Maeve. 'Anyway, I'm

not busy, so I can start without you, and later on we can meet and continue our investigation.'

So she told me her plans and I went back to work.

* * *

Maeve was already waiting in the cool, dark kitchen. It was strange being there in the middle of the night. There were no pots bubbling on the stove, no Cook giving orders, and no busy kitchen maids.

'At last!' whispered Maeve. 'Where were you?'

'Sorry. Nellie took ages to fall asleep, and I didn't dare move until I could hear her snoring.'

'It doesn't matter. I've already made a good start.'

She held out a beautiful leather-bound notebook. 'Here,' she said. 'I've interviewed all the witnesses.'

I opened the book, and on the first page, in Maeve's beautiful handwriting it said - *Witness statements*. Underneath, she had written what people had told her. I could see that Maeve had put in a lot of work, but unfortunately she hadn't discovered anything I didn't already know.

'I got nearly everyone,' she said. 'But Mrs Bailey looked very cross when she saw me with the notebook, so I didn't dare ask her.'

I smiled. Maeve isn't afraid of much, but Mrs Bailey had been very scary ever since the food started to disappear.

'The next page is for suspects,' she said, but when I checked, all it said was the single word '*Suspects*', and the rest was blank.

'Don't worry,' she said brightly. 'Even Sherlock Holmes needs a bit of time to solve a case.'

'What's that?' I asked, seeing something poking out of her pocket.

'I brought a magnifying glass from Uncle Joss's study.'

'For what?'

'I haven't made up my mind yet, but

Sherlock Holmes always has one, and I'm sure it'll be useful for something. Anyway, while I was waiting I had a walk around the passageway to survey the scene.'

'That can't have taken long,' I said. The passageway wasn't long or wide like the ones upstairs.

She ignored my comment. 'I think it's best if we watch from just outside the kitchen door. That's where all the action seems to be. Let's take some chairs from the dining hall and we can get into position.'

We each got a chair, and placed them outside the open kitchen door. For a long time, neither of us said anything,

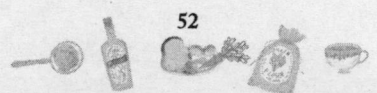

and the only sound was the ticking of the kitchen clock, and the occasional squeak and rattle as someone turned over in their iron bed.

After a while I yawned. 'Do we have to stay here for the *whole* night? It's cold – and a little bit boring.'

'Detectives can't worry about the cold,' said Maeve. 'They have to be clever and strong and patient – and anyway, something will probably happen soon.'

I wasn't sure I actually wanted something to happen, but I decided not to say this to the brave and confident girl beside me. I wrapped Mam's shawl tighter around my shoulders and tried

to think about nice things like summer days, and playing in the fields with my little brothers and sisters.

When I thought I couldn't stand it any more, I leaned over to see the clock, and saw that only twenty minutes had gone by. When I was asleep in my bed, the whole night went by in a flash, so it was hard to understand how slowly it could go when I was awake.

Then Maeve started to yawn too. 'Maybe this isn't such a good idea,' she said. 'I have a very busy day tomorrow. I've got a piano lesson in the morning, and a dress fitting in the afternoon.'

I smiled. That sounded like a lovely relaxing day to me.

'So are we giving up and going to bed?'

'No! Sherlock Holmes never gave up, and neither will we. We will take turns to sleep. Maybe an hour each? Do you want to go first?'

'That's nice of you,' I said, as I curled up in my chair as best I could and closed my eyes. Wake me when...'

But I was asleep before I could finish the sentence.

* * *

'Wake up, Lily. Wake up. I think I heard something.'

I was confused. There was a grey light coming through the windows, and I could hear birds singing.

'Why didn't you wake me?'

'I fell asleep too,' she said.

'So if we were both asleep, there could have been a chorus of ghosts and thieves dancing around us all night?'

'I suppose so. I'm sorry, Lily. We weren't very good detectives. I think it might be nearly morning.'

I rubbed my eyes and looked at the clock.

'It's not *nearly* morning,' I said, jumping to my feet. 'For me and the other servants it is morning. What you heard must be Agnes and Delia getting up to make breakfast. Hurry up, we have to get out of here before anyone sees us.'

We quickly put the chairs back into the dining hall.

'Are we detectives any more?' I asked.

'Of course we are. We have to be patient, remember? Even Sherlock Holmes couldn't solve a case in a single night. I'll see you in the kitchen the same time tonight, and I'll have a plan.'

Then she ran upstairs and I went to my room and slipped into bed. Seconds later, Agnes was knocking on the door. 'Get up, girls. Time for another lovely day of work.'

Chapter Six

No matter how many times I polished the big marble staircase that day, I couldn't please Mrs Bailey. She kept finding bits I'd missed, and bits I'd smudged, and places where one of the dogs had left pawprints on bits I'd just had perfect. Usually at times like that, I'd grit my teeth and dream of bedtime, but that didn't help when I knew I wouldn't be seeing much of my bed until Maeve and I had solved the mystery of the ghost.

* * *

'This book is so good,' said Nellie when I finally got to bed. 'I could sit here and read all night to get to the end and find out what happens.'

I had taught Nellie to read, and usually that made me proud and happy, but now all I wanted was for her to put out the gaslight and settle down. I had my own book open in front of me, but I kept reading the same line over and over as I tried not to think about the long hours ahead.

After a while, Nellie noticed my exaggerated yawning.

'Oh, Lily,' she said, closing her book quickly. 'Look at me being so selfish, and you sound as if you are exhausted.'

She put out the light, jumped back into bed and pulled the covers over herself. 'Sweet dreams.'

'Goodnight, Nellie,' I said, wondering how I could dream when I wasn't going to sleep.

* * *

Maeve had two chairs all ready outside the kitchen door. 'I've had the best idea,' she said, holding one of Cook's mixing bowls towards me. 'Look!'

'It's flour, but I don't know what…'

'We're going to sprinkle it all along the passageway.'

'I'm not a real detective,' I said. 'But I can still work out what's going to happen if Mrs Bailey catches us doing

that.'

'Don't worry so much. We can sweep it all up before morning.'

'I've already done enough sweeping today, thank you very much.'

Now she looked embarrassed. 'I'm sorry, Lily,' she said. 'Don't worry. I'll do all the sweeping, and anyway, when we catch the ghost, or the thief, or whatever it is, everyone will be delighted, and they won't care if the floor is a bit messy.'

'So tell me your idea,' I said, too tired to argue any more about a messy floor.

'Well, last night, we both fell asleep, and that might happen again tonight – we're only young and can't stay awake

the way grown-ups do.'

'And?'

'And now, if we're asleep and some-one or something comes past, they'll leave footprints.'

'And we'll be able to see where they come from.'

'And, more important – we'll be able to see where they go. We can follow the prints and catch the thief.'

I had to admit it was a good idea, but then I began to see a problem.

'Do ghosts leave footprints? Maybe they just glide along without leaving any trace at all?'

I could see she didn't like this. 'No one knows for sure,' she said. 'Maybe

some ghosts leave footprints and others don't. Or maybe it isn't even a ghost. Anyway – this is the best idea I've had in ages, and if you don't like it you can go back to bed and I'll work on my own.'

Bed sounded tempting, but I wasn't giving up that easily – and I didn't want to let my friend down. 'Come on,' I said. 'Let's get started.'

I took the bowl from her and began to sprinkle the flour all along the stone slabs.

When we had sprinkled the whole place with flour, we walked carefully along the edge of the passageway, being careful not to disturb the snowy

white carpet we had made. We sat down on our chairs, made ourselves as comfortable as we could, and began to wait.

At first, Maeve told ghost stories, but that scared me too much, so then she told me about her last trip to Dublin, and all the fine things she had seen there.

'Dublin!' I sighed. 'It must be a magical place.'

'I'm sure you'll get there one day.'

'Never! There will never be a day when a poor housemaid like me will be able to travel all the way to Dublin. I'll have to be happy here in Sligo for the rest of my life.'

It was still dark outside. My neck was stiff and my feet were cold. I sat up quickly and nearly fell off the chair.

'What?' said Maeve, opening her eyes. 'What happened? Did you hear something.'

'No. I woke up because I was so uncomfortable.'

Then Maeve grabbed my arm. 'Look!' she said, pointing at the ground near us.

In the dim light it took me a second to work out what I was seeing. It was a print in the flour – the print of a tiny bare foot.

Even though it was like the prints

my little sisters left when they ran in the muddy yard, this one scared me. I wasn't happy with the idea that someone – or something – had slipped past while Maeve and I were sleeping.

'I'm scared,' I said.

'Don't be,' said Maeve, putting her arm around me. 'Whatever it is, it's only little. It can't hurt us.'

'What if it's a ghost? My mam says there's no such thing as ghosts, but sometimes our neighbours tell stories that would…'

'I nearly forgot,' said Maeve picking up the magnifying glass she had left on the floor under her chair. 'I can use this to look for clues.'

She bent down and examined the footprint carefully, squinting with one eye.

Then I laughed and forgot that I was scared. 'We don't need a magnifying glass,' I said. 'Look over there.'

We looked at the trail of tiny footprints leading into the kitchen, and then back out, and along the passage-way.

'Let's follow them,' said Maeve. 'Keep in close to the wall so we don't ruin the trail by walking on it.'

I held her hand as we edged our way along. We went past Johanna's room, past mine and Nellie's room, and then ... the trail ended with half a footprint

under the closed door.

'Delia?' I said, confused. 'This is Delia's room.'

'Do you think these are her footprints?'

'Definitely not – she's got huge big feet – she wanted to try on my boots one time and could barely fit her toes in.'

'So whoever – or whatever – made these marks is in there with her?'

I nodded. Part of me wanted to run away, but I knew I couldn't do that. What if a ghost or a tiny thief had come to take Delia away? It didn't matter how scared Maeve and I were, we had to save her.

'Should we knock on the door?' I asked.

'No. If there's a ghost — we have to surprise it, in case it...'

'In case it what?'

'Oh, it doesn't matter. Just open the door.'

'Why me?'

I looked at Maeve, and saw that she was scared too. 'You open the door,' I said. 'And I'll hold your hand.'

The door creaked a little, but there was no other sound. The room was in darkness, but as Maeve pushed the door further, the light from the passageway fell across the bed.

Delia was sound asleep, and curled up in her arms was a tiny little girl.

Chapter Seven

Maeve squeezed my hand, but I wasn't afraid. If that was a ghost in Delia's bed, it was a very small, darling little one. I was confused, why would there be a child – or a ghost – in Delia's bed?

'Delia,' I whispered. 'Delia. Wake up.'

Delia didn't stir, but the child-ghost opened her eyes. She seemed surprised to see Maeve and me, and stretched out a tiny hand to tug at Delia's hair. I'm not an expert on ghosts, but now I

could see for sure that this wasn't one. This was a very small, very frightened little girl.

'Shush, child,' said Delia without opening her eyes. 'It's not morning yet. Go back to sleep.'

Once more the child tugged her hair. 'I'm not telling you ag...' Now Delia opened her eyes. It took her a second to notice Maeve and me standing in the doorway, and when she did, she looked absolutely terrified – almost as if she had seen a ghost! She quickly pulled a blanket over the child's head. I began to wish that it was a ghost in the bed with her, as the child would surely be smothered.

'Miss Maeve?' said Delia. 'Lily? What are you doing here in the middle of the night?'

'We saw the child in bed with you,' I said.

'What child?' she asked innocently. 'I don't know what you're talking about.'

I pulled Maeve fully into the room and took a step towards the bed. Delia held out her hand to stop me.

'Go away,' she said. 'Please go away. You didn't see anything. You must be dreaming or sleepwalking or something.'

Then the little girl popped her head out from under the blanket. 'Shhh, Dede,' she whispered. 'No talking at

night-time, remember?'

I smiled at the little creature, as Delia began to cry. 'Please,' she said as tears streamed down her face. 'Please don't tell anyone, Lily. I beg you not to say a word.'

She was talking to me, but looking at Maeve. I went and sat on the end of the bed, and Maeve stood next to me.

'Tell me, Delia,' I said. 'Tell me what's going on. Who is this little girl?'

For a long time, Delia didn't say anything, as she used the sleeve of her nightgown to wipe her tears. The little girl patted and stroked her, looking close to tears herself.

Finally, Delia sat up and blew her

nose. 'Can you close the door, please?' she said.

Maeve closed the door, and then came back over and sat on the bed. It was a tiny bed, and getting a bit crowded, but I don't think anyone minded.

The room was eerie without the light coming from the passageway, and it took me a few minutes to get used to the silvery glow from the moon through the trees outside.

'This is my little sister, Jane,' said Delia.

'Hello, Jane,' I said, smiling at her. 'How are you?'

She smiled back at me, not looking

scared any more. 'I'm very well,' she said politely. 'But I'm not supposed to talk to you, or to anyone 'cept Dede. I'm supposed to hide.'

She was a very sweet girl, and she reminded me a lot of my own two sisters. I wanted to pick her up and hug her, but now wasn't the time.

'What is she doing here?' asked Maeve.

'My dad and my brothers are gone to England to look for work,' said Delia. 'There was only Mam and Jane left at home, but Mam is...' Tears came to her eyes again, and she wiped them away before continuing. 'Mam is very sick. She can't take care of Jane ...

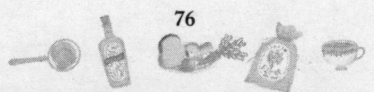

if I didn't do something, I was afraid the two of them would end up in the workhouse. So last week, in the middle of the night I walked home and got Jane and brought her here. No one saw us coming through the servants' tunnel and through the side door ... and I'm sorry about the food I took, but she's always hungry and ... sometimes when I'm asleep she sneaks into the kitchen. I tell her not to, but I think she's half asleep when she does it. I'm sorry about the fright Ita got ... and ... oh, Miss Maeve, please don't tell anyone. As soon as Mam is better, Jane can go home again, but until then she has to stay here with me ... there isn't

anywhere else for her to go.'

I felt sorry for the poor little scrap. She must have been so lonely and scared all the hours when Delia had to be at work.

'She doesn't have to hide,' said Maeve. 'Everyone knows how kind Aunt Mary is. I can explain to her, and I'm sure she will let Jane stay here with you.'

'No!' said Delia. 'I know Lady Mary is very kind, but I don't think she'll let Jane stay. What if Lily's mam got sick, could she bring her brothers and sisters to Lissadell? And what about the other servants? Everyone has problems, and Lady Mary can't fix them all.'

'I can ask her,' said Maeve.

'And if she says no?' said Delia. 'Then what will happen?'

No one had a good answer to this.

'Delia,' I said gently. 'I'm very sorry for you and Jane and your mam, but you can't go on like this. Jane has to eat, and Cook is watching the kitchen like a hawk. Before long, she'll find out and then…'

'I know what to do,' said Maeve. 'No one cares where I go or what I eat. I can easily get all the food I want and bring it here for Jane.'

'You'd do that for us?' said Delia.

'Of course I would,' said Maeve. 'I'm happy to help – and besides, I like a bit of

excitement.'

'So if food isn't going missing any more,' I said to Delia. 'And Jane stays nice and quiet, and doesn't go wandering in the night, you could probably get away with it for a few more days, and maybe then your mam will be better and everything will be all right.'

But Delia wasn't listening to me. She was staring at Maeve as if she were the most wonderful person she had ever seen. For a second I felt a small bit jealous – most people are happy to help, but when you're rich, it's so much easier!

Chapter Eight

For the next few days, Maeve did exactly as she promised, sneaking to the basement with baskets of fine food. Once I went with her, and it was lovely to see how little Jane's face lit up when she took the cloth off the basket and saw the many treats inside.

Whenever I got the chance, I sneaked into Delia's room to play with Jane for a few minutes. Usually she was sitting on the bed, playing quietly with her tiny rag doll, but her little face lit up when she saw me, bringing tears to

my eyes with how brave she was being.

'Has Jane been crying at night?' asked Maeve one day, when I met her going up the servants' stairs after bringing food to Jane.

'No,' I said. 'She's been a perfect, quiet little lamb.'

'I suppose she's getting used to her strange new life.'

'That's part of it, I think – but also she isn't alone as much as she was before you and I found out about her. Delia had to be so careful, she was only able to grab a small few minutes every day to spend with Jane – and the poor child must have been terrified. Now she's got you and me as well, so

things are easier for her, and she can sleep soundly at night.'

'Are Mrs Bailey and Cook still suspicious?'

'I don't think so. Now that Jane is quiet, and food isn't going missing, everyone is getting on with their lives. Thanks to you, everything is back to normal.'

'Thanks to both of us,' said Maeve, smiling.

* * *

'Why does this house have to have so many mirrors?' I groaned. 'I smell like the kitchen, and I don't know if my fingers will ever be clean again.'

Mrs Bailey had asked Nellie and me

to clean all the mirrors, using vinegar and old newspapers. It was a job I hated, but patient Nellie never complained – even now, when we had to stand on chairs to do the dining room mirror, that was so big it wouldn't fit in any room in my house. Nellie was good at getting on with things.

'We need more newspapers,' she said, throwing another wet crumpled one into the bucket beside us.

'I'll go,' I said.

'You've been up and down the stairs ten times already today,' she said. 'Why don't I go this time?'

'No,' I said, jumping down from my

chair. 'I don't mind – honestly.'

She gave me a funny look, and I felt bad. I hated keeping secrets from my friend. I wished I could tell her that every time I went downstairs, I spent a small few minutes keeping Jane company. I knew Nellie would never tell a soul, but Delia had begged me not to tell her – and so I didn't.

* * *

Early next morning, Delia knocked on my bedroom door.

'Get up, Lily and Nellie,' she said. 'Hurry! You're needed out here.'

Delia was often sent to wake Nellie and me, but now she seemed even more rushed than usual.

'What is it?' I said, jumping out of bed so quickly, I didn't even notice the cold stone under my bare feet. Had someone discovered Jane? Was the poor little girl going to be sent away?

'Countess Markievicz is coming later today,' said Delia when I opened the door. 'She didn't tell anyone until late last night, and Mrs Bailey is having conniptions.'

I was relieved that Jane hadn't been discovered, but this was still bad news for Nellie and me.

'Oh no,' I sighed. 'We'll be running around all day getting her room and dressing room ready.'

'Miss Maeve will be happy,' said

Nellie, sitting up and rubbing her eyes.

'You're right,' I said. How could I have forgotten Maeve in all of this? She hardly ever saw her mother, and every visit was like a rare gift. I knew Maeve would have no time for me today – but I didn't mind – everyone needs time with their mam.

'Well, I can't stay chatting for the day,' said Delia. 'Cook wants to make a special meal for the Countess, so there won't be any rest for me either. Get a move on girls.'

And then she was gone, hurrying along the corridor as if she were being chased by a real ghost.

It was very late before Nellie and I were free to go to bed.

'Good night,' she said, pulling the covers over her.

I was already in my nightgown, and almost asleep on my feet, but I couldn't settle down.

'Good night, Nellie,' I said. 'I'll be in bed in a minute, but first I have to ... I have to ... get a drink of water.'

I checked that the passageway was clear, and then hurried to Delia's room. 'It's only me – Lily,' I said, so she wouldn't be frightened, as I closed the door softly behind me.

Delia was sitting on her bed, with

her little sister sobbing quietly in her arms. My heart broke as I thought of my own sisters, who could waken the dead with their crying when they were upset. Poor Jane had learned how to cry quietly.

'The poor lamb,' I said. 'Is she sick?'

Delia shook her head.

'No one played with me,' sobbed the child. 'I was all on my own.'

'Are you hungry?' I asked.

'She had plenty to eat,' said Delia. 'Miss Maeve didn't forget her. She brought lots of food this morning, but she had no time to play and chat the way she usually does. And Cook had me running around in circles, so I

could only drop in for a minute.'

'And I didn't have time to check on her either,' I said. 'I'm sorry, Jane, but tomorrow will be different, I promise. We'll come and see you so often you'll be fed up of us. You'll wish…'

Before I could finish the sentence, the door opened again. Delia reached for the blanket to cover Jane, but then I saw who was there.'

'It's all right, Delia,' I said. 'It's only Maeve.'

But as Maeve came in and closed the door behind her, I saw that she was out of breath and had a worried look on her face. 'Mother knows about Jane,' she said. 'She's on her way

– I ran down the stairs ahead of her –
but she'll be here any minute!'

Chapter Nine

Delia pulled Jane closer to her. 'How does the Countess know?' she said. 'Who told her?'

I'd been wondering that too, but one look at my friend's face told me all I needed to know.

'I told her,' said Maeve quietly.

'You *what?*' Like all the servants, Delia treated Maeve with respect, but now she looked as if she wanted to kill her. 'It's so easy for rich people like you – you're not afraid of the workhouse, or starving or anything. You lot…'

Maeve was starting to look sick, and I was afraid Delia would get in trouble if she said any more.

'Why did you tell, Maeve?' I asked.

'I thought it was the right thing to do. We don't know how long your mother will be sick for, Delia. We're all doing our best, but things can't go on like this. Jane should be free to go outside and laugh and run around like my little cousins do. It's not fair keeping her hidden away like this.'

'Of course it's not fair,' said Delia angrily. 'But I don't have any choice, do I?'

'Mother will know what to do,' said Maeve. 'She will make things right.'

'Are you sure?' I asked.

Maeve nodded. 'Mother was talking with Uncle Joss this evening, and he was laughing, and talking about what she was like when she was a little girl. He reminded her of what used to happen when she went out walking in the winter with her sister Eva.'

'What happened?' I asked.

'Every time they met a poor person who was cold, Mother and Eva gave them their own coats to keep them warm. Sometimes they got into trouble, but Grandmother knew they were being kind, so she wasn't very cross.'

'That was nice of your mother,' I said.

'I know,' said Maeve. 'And every

one of Uncle Joss's stories was about Mother doing something kind for poor people – and that's when I knew she would never let anything bad happen to Jane. As soon as Uncle Joss went out to talk to Mr Kilgallon, I took my chance, and told Mother everything.'

Delia still wasn't happy. 'It was *my* secret,' she said. 'You shouldn't have…'

But before she could finish her sentence, the door opened, and in the shadowy passageway, I could see Maeve's mother, Countess Markievicz!

She stepped into the room, and little Jane's mouth dropped open at the sight of the fine lady, in her fancy dress and jewellery. Delia looked about

ready to die.

'Dear girl,' said the Countess to Delia. 'Sometimes secrets are too big for young people. Sometimes they have to be shared. Maeve did the right thing when she told me.'

I could see that Delia didn't agree, but who would dare to argue with the Countess?

The Countess walked towards the bed, and Jane began to cry, pulling the covers over her head.

The Countess stopped walking. 'I suppose I am a little bit frightening,' she said, not seeming to mind very much. 'Anyway, I presume you are Delia?'

Delia nodded, and the Countess continued. 'I am very sorry to hear about your mother – and I am sorry that you felt you had to hide your little sister here in your bedroom. Don't worry, though – everything is going to be all right.'

And something about the way she said the words, made me know that she was telling the truth.

Chapter Ten

A few minutes later, Delia had told Countess Markievicz all about her sick mother, and had answered her questions about doctors and medicine. (This didn't take long, as Delia's family couldn't afford either.) Jane was peeping her head out from under the blanket, and laughing at the funny faces Maeve was making, and Delia didn't look angry or scared any more.

Then I heard footsteps coming along the passageway. 'Maybe it's a ghost,' said Maeve, laughing.

But I was worried – our little 'ghost' was right here in front of us, so who could it be?

Then the door opened and Mrs Bailey appeared, and I became very, very worried.

'What on earth is all this racket? I thought we were finished with this nonsense!'

And then she saw the Countess!

I felt sorry for poor Mrs Bailey. Her face went pale, and she wrapped her shawl tighter around herself, almost as if she wanted to disappear - as if she could somehow pretend not to be standing in front of a fine lady, while wearing a long nightgown and a frilly

night cap.

'Ah, Mrs Bailey,' said the Countess calmly. 'I'm glad you are here. I gather you didn't know about this young visitor?'

'Indeed I did not,' said Mrs Bailey, looking at Jane. 'If I had known, I would have informed Sir Josslyn and Lady Mary at once.'

'It's Delia's little sister,' said Maeve. 'Don't be cross, Mrs Bailey – their mother is sick and she didn't have anywhere else to go.'

Mrs Bailey's face made me think she was very cross, but how could she say a word with the Countess there?

'Don't worry,' said the Countess. 'I

know she can't stay here after tonight. I promise she will be leaving first thing in the morning.'

At these words, Mrs Bailey looked happier, but Jane and Delia began to cry.

'Mother!' said Maeve. 'You can't!'

'Calm down, dear,' said the Countess. 'You don't think I'd put the poor child out on the street? Delia can take her home – and she can stay there until her mother is well again – no matter how long that takes.'

'How are we to manage without Delia?' asked Mrs Bailey.

'I'm sure with your skill as a house-keeper, you will be able to keep things

running smoothly until her return. I myself will be here until lunchtime tomorrow, and I can help out if needs be.'

I put my hand over my mouth to cover my giggles. Countess Markievicz was a very unusual woman, and I knew she once worked in a soup kitchen in Dublin, but the thought of her peeling potatoes in the kitchen at Lissadell was hilarious.

'No need for that,' said Mrs Bailey quickly. Then she turned to Delia and spoke in a gentler voice. 'I'm sorry about your mother,' she said. 'You go on home tomorrow, and we'll manage fine until you get back.'

'But...' Delia stopped talking, but I guessed she was thinking the same as I would in her situation. A few days or weeks at home would be lovely, but without my wages, how would the family eat?

'I will make sure that your wages are paid as usual,' said the Countess. 'And I will send some medicine, and the finest doctor in the county. I'm sure your mother will be fighting fit in no time.'

Now Delia cried even more, but I could see they were happy tears.

I yawned, suddenly realising how late it must be, and how little time in bed I was going to have.

'Bedtime for everyone, I think,' said the Countess. 'Maybe it would be best if Delia and her little sister were to sleep upstairs in one of the guest rooms.'

Mrs Bailey looked horrified. She opened her mouth, and for the first time ever, I saw that she had no words to say.

'You surely can't expect them to squash in this tiny bed for another night, can you?' said the Countess.

Once again I wanted to laugh. Didn't she know what poor families we all came from? Most of us had never slept on our own before coming to Lissadell.

'I'm very grateful to you for everything, Madame,' said Delia. 'But I couldn't spend the night upstairs. I wouldn't sleep a wink, and that's for sure.'

'As you wish,' said the Countess, turning towards the door. 'I'll come down in the morning and we can make all the arrangements. I will take Joss's car and drive you home myself. Your mother will have a wonderful surprise when she sees you. Good night everyone.'

* * *

'Where were you?' asked Nellie when I got back to our room. 'I was worried – I thought that maybe the ghost was

back and had hurt you, and I was just running out to help you, but then I heard the Countess's voice, and I realised I was more scared of her than of any little ghost, and...'

'Oh, Nellie, I'm sorry,' I said. 'There was never a ghost, it was only Delia's little sister, and...'

The two of us settled down in our beds, and I told her the whole story, making her laugh by putting on everyone's voices.

'That was like a story in one of the nursery books,' she said when I was finished. 'And it has a happy ending and everything. Now let's go to sleep, it'll be morning before we know it.'

'There's one more thing, Nellie,' I said. 'I ... I'm sorry I didn't tell you about Jane before. I really wanted to but, Delia begged me not to, and...'

'It's all right,' she said. 'I understand.'

I reached out my hand and held hers for a moment. I knew how lucky I was to have a good friend like Nellie.

* * *

On my day off, I didn't care how tired I was as I hurried home to see my lovely family. As usual, my little sisters ran to hug me, and my brothers smiled quietly, trying to look as if they didn't care if I was there or not.

'Darling girl,' said Mam, as she came out, wiping her hands on her apron.

'How are you? Have you any news for your dear old mam?'

'There has been a *bit* of excitement,' I said.

She gave me one of her wonderful hugs, the kind that made me forget about all my cares and troubles.

'Come inside,' she said when she finally let me go. 'Sit yourself by the fire and tell me everything.'

And that's what I did.

Friends Lily and Nellie work hard as housemaids in Lissadell. And yet these are days filled with friendship, fun, and even madcap bicycle rides with Maeve, daughter of the famous Republican, Countess Markievicz. But Nellie is all alone in the world; she grew up in the workhouse, where she was separated from her sisters. Lily longs to help her, but how can she?

On your bookmarks, get set, read!

Well hello there! We are

Overjoyed that you have joined our celebration of

Reading books and sharing stories, because we

Love bringing books to you.

Did you know, we are a charity dedicated to celebrating the

Brilliance of reading for pleasure for everyone, everywhere?

Our mission is to help you discover brand new stories and

Open your mind to exciting worlds and characters, from

Kings and queens to wizards and pirates to animals and adventurers and so many more. We couldn't

Do it without all the amazing authors and illustrators, booksellers and bookshops, publishers, schools and libraries out there –

And most importantly, we couldn't do it all without . . .

You!

Changing lives through a love of books and shared reading.

World Book Day is a registered charity funded by publishers and booksellers in the UK & Ireland.

illustrated by *Rob Biddulph*

SPONSORED BY

WORLD BOOK DAY

Share a story

From breakfast to bedtime, there's always time to discover and share stories together. You can . . .

1 Take a trip to your local bookshop

Brimming with brilliant books and helpful booksellers to share awesome reading recommendations, you can also enjoy booky events with your favourite authors and illustrators.

Find your local bookshop in the UK or Ireland:
booksellers.org.uk/bookshopsearch

2 Join your local library

That wonderful place where the hugest selection of books you could ever want to read awaits – and you can borrow them for FREE! Plus expert advice and fantastic free family reading events.

Find your local library:
librariesireland.ie/find-your-local-library

3 Check out the World Book Day website

Looking for reading tips, advice and inspiration? There is so much to discover at **worldbookday.com**, packed with fun activities, audiobooks, videos, competitions and all the latest book news galore. There's a special Irish page at **worldbookday.com/about-us/ireland/**